This book belongs to

_____

BRADY BRADY

Game Time Collection

BRADY BRADY

Game Time Collection

Written by **Mary Shaw**
Illustrated by **Chuck Temple**

Scholastic Canada Ltd.
Toronto New York London Auckland Sydney
Mexico City New Delhi Hong Kong Buenos Aires

Scholastic Canada Ltd.
604 King Street West, Toronto, Ontario M5V 1E1, Canada

Scholastic Inc.
557 Broadway, New York, NY 10012, USA

Scholastic Australia Pty Limited
PO Box 579, Gosford, NSW 2250, Australia

Scholastic New Zealand Limited
Private Bag 94407, Botany, Manukau 2163, New Zealand

Scholastic Children's Books
Euston House, 24 Eversholt Street, London NW1 1DB, UK

www.scholastic.ca

Library and Archives Canada Cataloguing in Publication

Shaw, Mary, 1965-
[Novels. Selections]
Brady Brady game time collection / written by Mary Shaw ; illustrated
by Chuck Temple.

Contents: Brady Brady and the singing tree -- Brady Brady and the missed
Hatrick -- Brady Brady and the cranky kicker -- Brady Brady and the
ballpark bark -- Brady Brady and the cleanup hitters.
ISBN 978-1-4431-6371-2 (hardcover)

I. Temple, Chuck, 1962-, illustrator II. Shaw, Mary, 1965- Brady Brady
and the singing tree. III. Title.

PS8587.H3473A6 2018   jC813'.6   C2018-901056-8

Published by arrangement with Brady Brady Inc.

6 5 4 3 2 1   Printed in China 38   18 19 20 21 22

Contents

BRADY BRADY
and the Singing Tree

Brady was worried. His friend Elwood hadn't been very happy lately, and Brady was pretty sure he knew why.

Ever since Elwood had lumbered into the dressing room, twice as tall as the other kids, the Icehogs had called him "Tree." Tree liked his nickname way better than "Elwood." And he loved to play hockey, just for the fun of it.

Tree's dad LOVED hockey too, but for a different reason. He dreamed of Elwood becoming a big star one day and playing in the NHL. That seemed to be all that mattered to him. So, when Brady noticed that Tree was feeling down, it wasn't hard to figure out what was wrong.

Between games, Tree's dad always made him do sit-ups, push-ups, and laps. Tree hated running laps.

On the way to games, his dad talked hockey non-stop. Tree just wanted to listen to the radio.

Before games, while his friends played mini-sticks with a tapeball in the dressing room, Tree was usually with his dad. They sat in the stands watching other teams while his father pointed out what they were doing right or wrong.

At games, Tree — and everyone else — could hear his dad yelling at him.

"Skate faster!" "Keep your head up!" "Wake up out there!"

10

It was embarrassing. Sometimes Tree wanted to take his equipment off and forget about playing altogether. Couldn't his dad see that he just wanted to play hockey for the *fun* of it?

The Icehogs felt bad for Tree. Brady wanted to help, but he wasn't sure what to say. Then one day, he began to dream out loud as the Icehogs got dressed for a game. Pretty soon the rest of the team was dreaming too, even Tree.

"Wouldn't it be *great* to be a *woman* player in the NHL!" Tes exclaimed.

"Wouldn't it be *great* to get a *shutout* in the NHL!" chimed in Chester.

"Wouldn't it be **great** to score a ***hat trick*** in the NHL!" Brady added.

"Wouldn't it be **great** to **sing** in the NHL!" shouted Tree.

*"**WHAT?!?!?!?!**"* Everyone froze.

"Did you say, *'sing'* in the NHL?" Brady asked.

"Yeah, Brady Brady," said Tree. "I've always wanted to sing the anthem at an NHL game. Don't tell my dad."

With all of the daydreaming going on,
the Icehogs had to rush their team cheer.

*"We've got the power,
We've got the might,
Tree wants to be a singer,
And that's all right!"*

The Icehogs dashed out of the dressing room and, without another word, pushed Tree to center ice. The crowd fell silent. Nobody knew what was going on, especially Tree.

"You don't need to tell your dad," Brady whispered in his ear. "Show him."

"Brady Brady, I can't . . ."

Tree was suddenly left standing alone. He closed his eyes, lifted his chin, opened his arms wide . . . and began to sing.

Tree had the most *incredible* voice!

When he was finished, the crowd clapped and whistled. Both teams slapped their sticks on the ice. There had never been so much noise in the building.

Tree grinned from ear to ear. He looked into the stands for his dad.

His father was *not* grinning from ear to ear.

On the way home, Tree was reminded that he was a hockey player, not a singer. "No son of mine is trading a hockey stick for a microphone," his dad said gruffly.

Tree swallowed hard. "I *love* hockey, Dad, and I *want* to play, but only if I can have fun. And only if I can sing at all the Icehogs games. The coach already asked me, and I said yes."

Tree's father looked surprised. He started to object, but instead he said, "Well, if you feel that way I guess you may. But only if you work extra hard at practices."

Tree agreed, and they had a deal.

For a while everything was fine. Singing made Tree so happy that his hockey improved. This, of course, made his dad happy. Not only that, the Icehogs began to get a lot of attention, both on and off the ice. Everyone was talking about their great games and the kid who sang the anthem. Tree was even interviewed for the community paper.

Then one day, the coach made a surprise announcement. The Icehogs had been invited to skate between periods at a real NHL game!

It was a dream come true — for everyone except Tree. For Tree it was more like a nightmare.

"My dad will think this is my big chance to be a hockey star," he told Brady. "What if I goof up in front of everybody and disappoint him?"

"You won't," said Brady. "Besides, we'll all be out there. You'll be fine!"

No matter what Brady said, Tree was terrified.

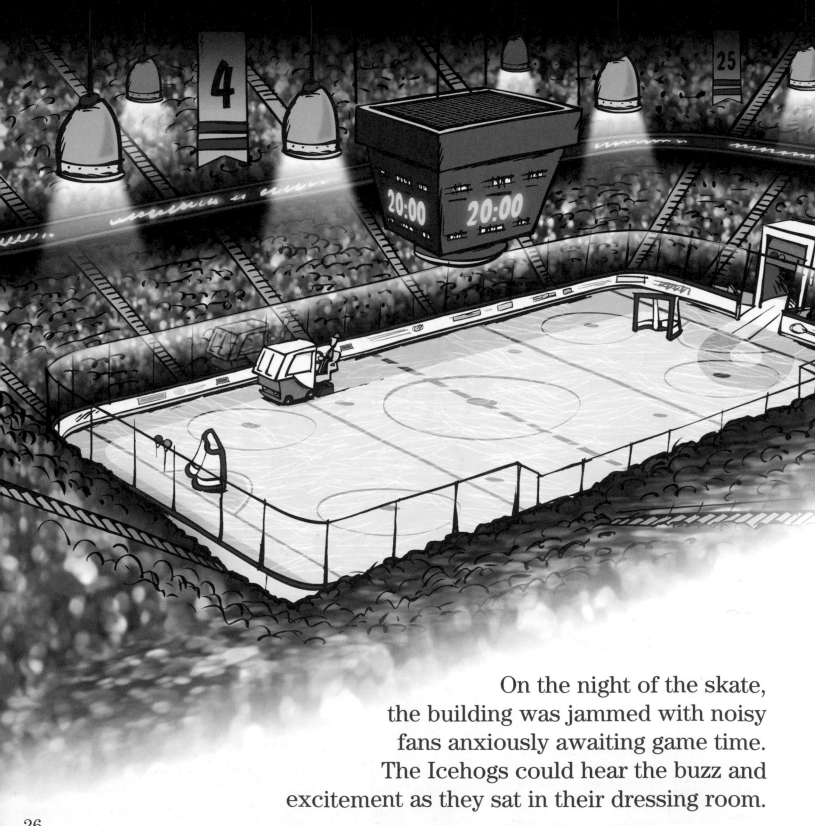

On the night of the skate,
the building was jammed with noisy
fans anxiously awaiting game time.
The Icehogs could hear the buzz and
excitement as they sat in their dressing room.

26

When a knock came at the door, they all jumped . . . especially Tree.

"They're ready for you!" the coach announced.

"But we're not supposed to come out until the first period ends!" said Brady.

"We aren't, but Tree is," beamed the coach. "I've been saving the best part till last. Tree is going to sing the opening anthem!"

Tree was stunned. He just stood there with his mouth hanging open.

"Well, what are you waiting for?" came a voice from behind. Tree turned to see his dad with a microphone in his hand. "I'll trade you this microphone for your stick. Son, you're the best anthem singer I know."

The noisy fans fell silent as the spotlight focused on center ice.
Stepping into the light, Tree closed his eyes, lifted his chin,
opened his arms wide . . . and began to sing.

As Tree bowed to the cheering crowd, he saw the face of his biggest fan, pressed up against the glass — grinning from ear to ear.

BRADY BRADY

and the Missed Hatrick

The snowplow roared past Brady's house. "Hooray!" he shouted. "Our street is plowed. Come on, Hatrick."

Brady bundled up in his warm clothes and headed to the shed to get his hockey stick.

"Whoa there, Brady Brady," his mom said, taking the hockey stick out of Brady's hand and trading it for a shovel. "The driveway needs to be cleared before your dad gets home."

"Aw, Mom," Brady groaned. The plow had left a huge heap of snow at the end of the driveway.

Brady got to work. He was about halfway finished when he spotted Chester and Tes walking toward him, carrying a hockey net.

"Up for a game of shinny?" Tes asked.

Brady didn't give it a second thought. Abandoning the shovel for his hockey stick, he joined his friends.

Their fun was interrupted by the sound of tires spinning. Brady's dad was stuck in the pile of snow at the end of the driveway.

"Oops! Gotta go," Brady told his friends and hurried off.

His dad did **not** look happy.

From then on, things went from bad to worse. His dad tripped over Brady's hockey bag and found wet, stinky equipment still inside. Brady had forgotten to air it out after yesterday's practice.

Brady's parents were upset that he was always rushing off to play instead of doing what he was supposed to be doing. They sent him to his room.

From his window, Brady could see the game of shinny still going on at the end of the street.

"Uh, Mom," Brady called.
"Should I take Hatrick for a walk before dinner?"

Brady's mom was thrilled that he was offering to walk the dog
without being asked. Hatrick loved walks as much as
Brady loved hockey.

When he reached the game, Brady tied Hatrick's leash to a lamppost and ran to join his friends. Hatrick whined and yelped, but no one paid any attention.

Brady didn't feel the cold as he chased the ball between both nets. But then it started to get dark and the game ended. Brady waved good-bye to his friends and ran home.

"Your dinner is getting cold," Brady's mom said, ruffling her son's hair. "At least Hatrick had a nice long walk." Brady's mouth dropped. His stomach felt like it had been punched.

"Say, where *is* Hatrick?" Brady's dad asked when he saw his son's face.

"I . . . I . . . tied him to a lamppost. I just played shinny for a couple of . . ." Brady's bottom lip started to quiver.

Brady's mom dragged him up the street in the dark. Under the streetlight, they found Hatrick's collar and leash but no Hatrick. Brady fought back tears as he and his mother walked the neighborhood, calling his dog over and over again.

Brady's dad and sister got into the car and drove around looking. There was no sign of Hatrick. Finally, they all had to give up and go home.

"Maybe he'll wander back on his own," Brady's mom said as she tucked Brady into bed. "I'll leave the shed door open for him, just in case."

Brady knew his mother was as worried as he was.

Brady stared at Hatrick's empty basket and listened to the winter wind howl. How could he have been so careless with his best buddy?

He tossed and turned all night.

Brady leapt out of bed in the morning to see if Hatrick had returned, but the look on his sister's face said it all.

Hatrick was still missing.

Brady felt too sick to eat breakfast. He couldn't look at his family. It was his fault they might never see their dog again.

His dad suggested going to the animal shelter to see if Hatrick had been brought in.

Brady rushed to go with him. It was better than doing nothing.

At the shelter, Brady ran from pen to pen, looking for his pal.

There, in the smallest cage, at the end of the last row, sat poor Hatrick. Brady tried to rattle the door open.

"Hold on, boy. I'll get you out of there," Brady whispered, sticking his fingers through the wire to touch his dog.

"Not so fast, son," said the attendant. "There's a shelter fee to get him back."

Brady's heart sank. He didn't have any money.

"I guess you'll be shoveling a lot of snow to earn that money," his father told him. "I'll **lend** it to you for now, but you'll have to repay me." He reached for his wallet. "I think that's the best way to teach you about responsibility."

He squeezed Brady's shoulder. "Besides, we can't leave our boy here, can we?"

"No, Dad," said Brady, handing the money over to the attendant. "And don't worry. I promise this will never happen again. One night without Hatrick was one night too many."

The man unlocked Hatrick's cage and winked at Brady. "Take good care of that dog," he said. "He looks like a real good friend."

Hatrick's tail whipped back and forth faster than Brady's best slapshot. "I will," said Brady, not even stopping to wipe Hatrick's slurpy kisses from his face. "Let's go home, boy."

That day, Brady shoveled his own and four of his neighbors' driveways.

His friends came by to see if he wanted to play road hockey, but Brady told them he was too busy. He wasn't sure he had the strength to hold a hockey stick, anyway. Besides, he had a promise to keep.

In bed that night, Brady had just enough energy left to wrap
his aching arms around Hatrick before he drifted off to dream
about snowdrifts and shovels, cages and money, wagging tails
and happy endings and, yes, hockey.

BRADY BRADY

and the Cranky Kicker

It was spring — time to put away the hockey skates and get out the football. Brady was looking forward to a game with his friends, until he found his ball, flattened, the way he had left it at the end of last season.

Old Mr. Luddy had let the air out of it before giving it back, just because it had gone into his garden . . . again.

Brady headed outside to where his dad was working in the yard.

"Dad, my friends and I are going to play football. Can you fix it?"

Brady's dad found the pump.

"Brady Brady," he said, "please be careful. I don't want Mr. Luddy getting upset again this year."

"We didn't upset him on purpose. Mr. Luddy is always cranky. Why do you think he is, Dad?"

"He and football don't mix, I guess. But he's a good neighbor. Try to keep the football out of his garden, okay?"

Brady promised, but he still thought Mr. Luddy was mean.

The kids were waiting on the empty lot when Brady arrived.

He was nervous as he set the ball down and lined up for the first big kick of the year. Brady had to keep the ball from going too far to the right — and into Mr. Luddy's yard.

Brady took a run, wound up, and missed the ball altogether. He fell flat on his back. His friends burst out laughing.

"Oops! I guess I shouldn't worry so much about where the ball is going."

"What's with all the racket out here!"

The kids jumped. It was Mr. Luddy. His face was red and he was very upset.

"Sorry, Mr. Luddy," Brady replied with a wave. "We'll try to keep it down."

Mr. Luddy scowled and walked away.

"Whatever we do," said Brady, "we better not kick the ball to the *right*!"

71

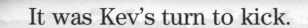

It was Kev's turn to kick.

As usual, he was talking too much when he hoofed the ball. It bounced along the ground, end over end, through the hedge, not stopping until it was in the middle of Mr. Luddy's vegetable patch.

The kids were terrified.

They played a game of Rock, Paper, Scissors to see who would retrieve the football.

Brady got stuck with the job.

As Brady reached down
to pick up his football,
a huge foot stomped on it.

"You kids are testing my patience," grumbled Mr. Luddy. "Next time, you won't get your football back!"

With that he kicked the ball *waaay* to the far end of the empty lot.

Kev retrieved the football and then joined his friends in a group huddle.

"We have to be more careful," Brady said.

"That's for sure! Mr. Luddy was furious," added Tes.

"Yeah, but did you see how far he kicked the ball?" asked Kev.

Tes was up next. Chester did a few calculations and helped her line up the kick.

Tes leapt into the air, twirled in a circle, landed, and booted the ball with all her might.

High and straight, it was the perfect kick. That is, until . . . a gust of wind blew it off course — to the *right*!

The ball landed with a thud up against
Mr. Luddy's basement window.

"Uh-oh," said Chester.
His teeth began to chatter.

"What do we do now?" asked Tes.

"This time," Brady whispered,
"we all go and get it."

They stepped around the hedge
and tiptoed toward the
back of the house.

79

Brady could hear his heart thumping as he bent to pick up his football. As he grabbed it, something shiny caught his eye.

"Cool!" said Brady. The basement was filled with trophies and football pictures. In one corner was the biggest trophy he had ever seen.

"**HEY!** What are you kids doing over there?"
Mr. Luddy yelled, coming up behind them.

Clutching his ball, Brady stood up
to face his neighbor.

81

"We're really sorry, sir," Brady said. "It was an accident. The wind blew the ball here — honest."

"Bah! The wind," Mr. Luddy huffed.

82

But then, something in the old man's face changed, and Brady wasn't afraid anymore.

"Mr. Luddy," he said, "did you win that big trophy down there? Dad said you and football don't mix, but I think you must love the game as much as we do."

Without a word, Mr. Luddy turned and walked away.

The kids didn't feel like playing anymore, especially since they couldn't get past the opening kick.

They were sitting in the field when Brady spotted his neighbor carrying the huge trophy and a photo album under his arm.

Mr. Luddy set the trophy down and puffed out his chest.

"This trophy is the Bronze Boot," he said. "I won it for being the best place-kicker in my league."

Mr. Luddy opened the album and showed them the pictures of himself when he was a young football hero. He told the kids his nickname had been Bull's Eye. Suddenly Mr. Luddy seemed sad.

He bent to gather up his things and knocked over the trophy. Brady picked it up to see if it was okay.

"Don't worry, Brady," said Mr. Luddy. "This trophy is nothing but bad luck, anyway."

"Bad luck!" Brady gasped. "How could that be?"

"After I won the Bronze Boot, our team went to the championship game. We were behind by a point and I was sent in to kick the winning field goal. The fans chanted my name. *'Bull's Eye! Bull's Eye! Bull's Eye!'* It was a sure thing . . . or so I thought." Mr. Luddy closed his eyes. "Like always, I kicked it straight and far. It was the *perfect* kick."

"But just then, a big gust of wind blew it off course. It went to the *right* of the goalpost. I had lost the game."

Mr. Luddy opened his eyes. "After that, I never played football again."

"Mr. Luddy!" cried Brady. "Would you like to play now?
You're the best football player we've ever met.
You could teach us how to play football for real!"

The kids all nodded in agreement.

"I'll teach you on one condition," said Mr. Luddy with a wink. "We spend some time on kicking first. You kids need a lot of work, especially if my garden is going to survive!"

"Deal!" Brady replied, shaking his neighbor's hand.

Mr. Luddy joined the kids in a huddle.
They yelled their team cheer at the top of their lungs.

"We've got the power,
We've got the might,
Kick the football left . . .
When the wind is blowing right!"

BRADY BRADY

and the Ballpark Bark

The day that Brady had been waiting for had finally arrived. He grabbed his bat and glove and headed to the ballpark to meet his new baseball team.

His dog, Hatrick, was excited, too! He carried an old baseball in his mouth as he raced out the door with Brady.

Brady was the first to arrive and the first to get a Mudbugs uniform.
He chose his lucky number 4. As his teammates arrived, Brady
high-fived them and Coach handed out more shirts and caps.
Tree was a bit late. The only uniform left was a size extra-small.
It just wouldn't do.

"Here, take mine," Coach told him. "You'll never be able to swing a bat in that." He put the extra-small shirt in his sports bag. Everyone was happy — until the practice started.

Coach had them run bases to warm up. Hatrick ran too, but he got in the way and tripped Tes.

They threw balls at the fence to improve their accuracy, but Hatrick swiped them all.

No one had a chance to catch a single pop fly or grounder.

Coach was watching. "Brady Brady," he called. "I'm sorry. The dog better go home. He's a great fan, but he doesn't know much about baseball."

Brady led Hatrick home, shut him in the house, and hurried back to the park in time for batting practice.

Tes hit the ball into right field. Kev whacked his into left field.

Brady was up next. He tied his laces in a double knot and headed toward home plate.

He hit the dust off his cleats and took a practice swing. Coach tossed the ball, and Brady swung the bat with all his might.

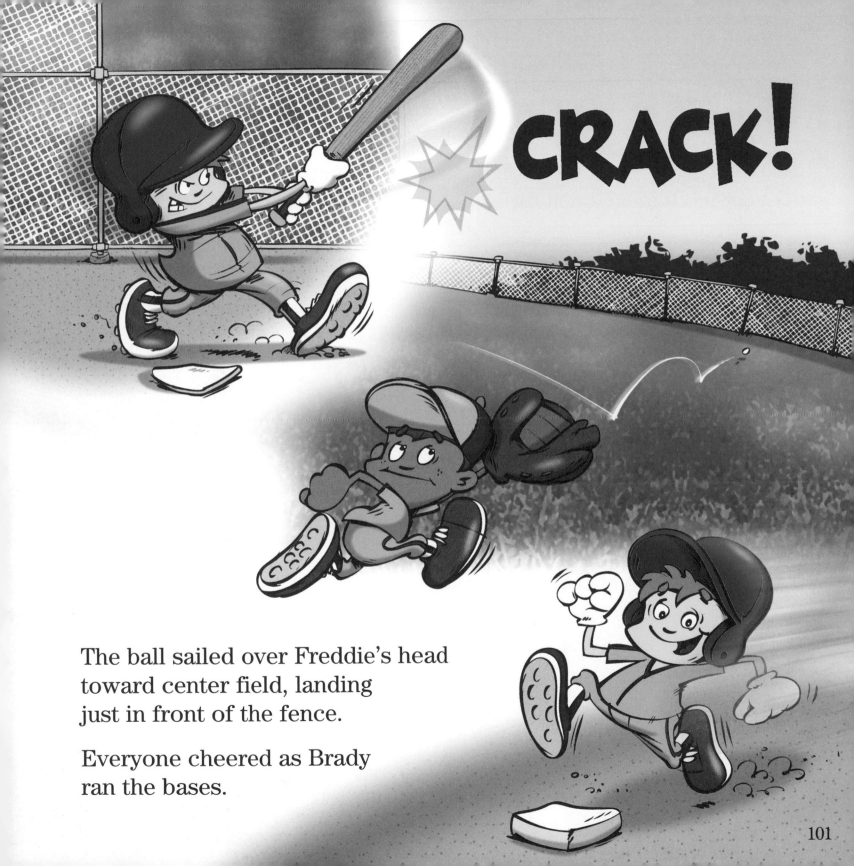

CRACK!

The ball sailed over Freddie's head toward center field, landing just in front of the fence.

Everyone cheered as Brady ran the bases.

Next, Coach pitched the ball to Tree. He swung hard — but **before** the ball even crossed home plate. "That's okay, Tree," Brady called from the dugout. Coach pitched again. Tree swung — but **after** the ball crossed home plate.

"You'll get it next time, Tree!" Brady called out again. But Tree missed every pitch that Coach threw.

"Don't worry, it's just a matter of timing," Coach explained to Tree as they walked to the dugout. "Opening day is coming up," he reminded his team. "Everyone has to be ready."

Tree was sure that Coach was talking about him.

"What am I going to do?" Tree said sadly, pulling his ball cap over his face. "I can't hit the ball to save my life!"

"I have a great idea!" Brady said. "We have one week to make you into the best hitter ever."

"WE?" the kids said in unison.

Brady Brady told the kids his plan. "Meet me in my backyard. We have our work cut out for us," he said, winking at Tree.

At home, Brady ran to the backyard shed. He gathered a garden glove, two pylons, and a burlap sack and made a baseball diamond.

Poor Hatrick barked to be let out, but Brady left him in the house so he wouldn't bother anyone.

The kids showed up and took their places on the field. As it turned out, they weren't really needed. Tree stood over the burlap sack swinging at every pitch Brady threw — but before or after the ball crossed the plate! Brady pitched until he thought his arm would drop off. Tree didn't hit a single ball.

When it got dark, Brady grabbed some flashlights from the
shed, and the kids took turns holding them. That way they
could work with Tree a little longer.

"Brady Brady, time to wrap it up,"
Brady's mom called from the window.

"It's late and Hatrick wants out. His barking is driving us
crrraaazy!"

Tree slumped to the ground. "It's no use," he said sadly. "We could
do this all summer, and I still wouldn't connect with the ball!"

Brady lay in bed that night trying to figure out a way to help his friend. Hatrick lay beside him with a baseball in his mouth.

"I know, buddy," Brady whispered. "I wish you could help too . . ."

Brady set up the backyard again the next day. Tree arrived, dragging his bat behind him.

"Maybe the bat's too short," Tes suggested.

"Maybe he's holding it too tight," said Chester.

"Maybe his shoes are on the wrong feet," added Kev.

Hatrick barked wildly from inside the house, but no one paid any attention.

Tree took his place over the burlap sack.

He didn't have any luck for the rest of the day. He was starting to panic.

After the kids left, Brady and Tree were trying a few last pitches when the back door opened. "Brady Brady," his dad shouted. "Hatrick needs company. He's been inside, barking, all day."

Hatrick ran up to Brady with the baseball in his mouth.

"Not now, boy," Brady told him. "Tree has to practice some more."

Hatrick sat by the fence, watching.

Tree shouldered the bat, and Brady threw him a straight pitch.
As the ball crossed the plate, Hatrick gave a sharp bark. Startled,
Tree swung. **Thwack!**

The ball sailed over the fence. Tree rubbed his eyes to make sure he hadn't imagined the incredible hit.

"Way to go, Tree!" Brady said. "Do it again!"

Tree got set for the next pitch. As the ball crossed the plate, Hatrick barked loudly. Tree swung, and again, the ball sailed out of the yard.

"What's gotten into you?" Brady asked.

"I guess I owe it to you and all this practice," Tree said, beaming. "Oh, and Hatrick, cheering me on."

"That's it!" Brady cried. "It *is* Hatrick! He's telling you when to swing!"

Brady put Hatrick in the house, then pitched to his friend, just like before. Tree went back to his old ways — swing and a miss, swing and a miss.

Brady called Hatrick back outside. Right on cue, Hatrick barked, and Tree crushed the ball over the fence. Tree and Hatrick sent ball after ball out of the yard. The timing was perfect. The season opener was tomorrow!

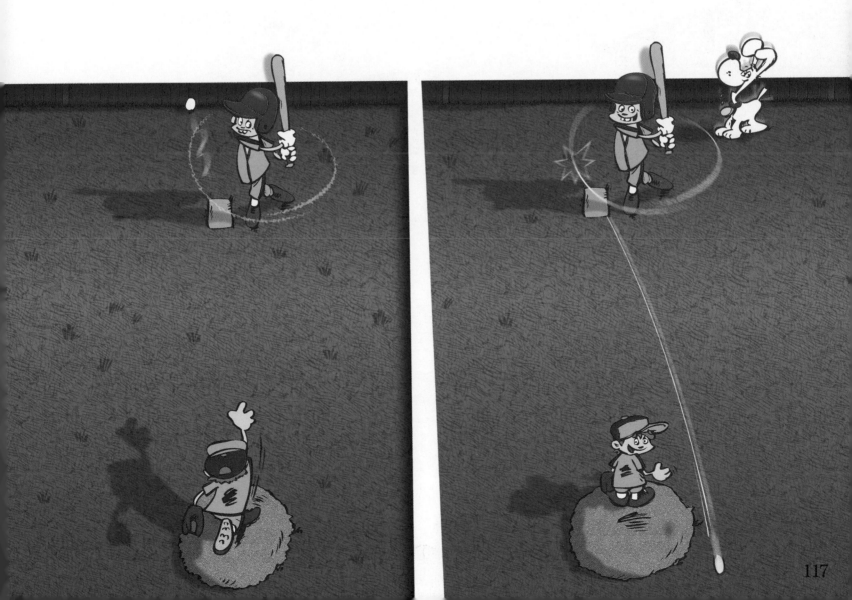

Opening day was filled with the excited chatter of fans and the smell of hot dogs.

Tree sat nervously in the dugout, making circles in the dust with his cleats until it was his turn to bat.

"You can do it," Brady said, patting Tree on the back. "With a little help from your friend." He pointed at the fence behind home plate.

There sat Hatrick, wagging his tail.

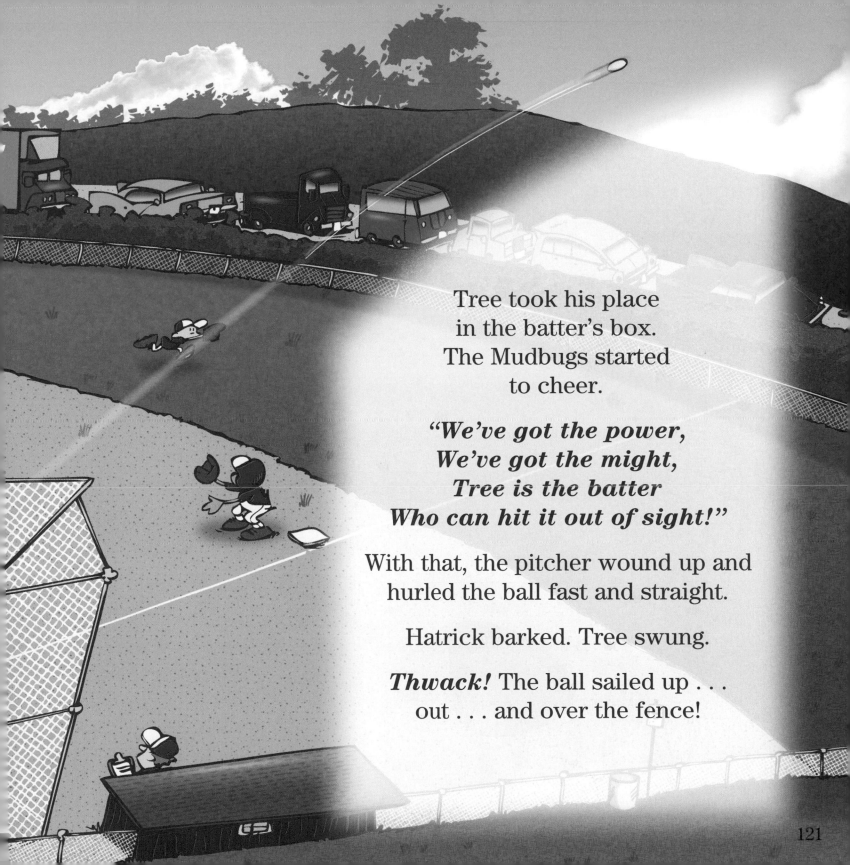

Tree took his place
in the batter's box.
The Mudbugs started
to cheer.

*"We've got the power,
We've got the might,
Tree is the batter
Who can hit it out of sight!"*

With that, the pitcher wound up and
hurled the ball fast and straight.

Hatrick barked. Tree swung.

Thwack! The ball sailed up . . .
out . . . and over the fence!

121

"Great game, Mudbugs!" Coach said, as they all slurped on treats in the dugout. "I think we're going to have an interesting season."

He reached into his sports bag for the leftover extra-small uniform and put it on Hatrick.

Hatrick, the Mudbugs' new mascot, couldn't have agreed more.

BRADY BRADY

and the Cleanup Hitters

April was a busy time of year. It was when Brady had to clean out his closet and recycle the stuff he no longer used.

"Brady Brady, your room is a pigsty!" His mom exclaimed. "Time for a spring cleanup."

His mom called it spring cleanup. Brady called it a waste of time. After all, April was also the start of the baseball season and he had better things to do. He couldn't wait to get out and play.

Even with Hatrick's help, there was just too much to sort.

While Brady rummaged through his closet, Hatrick rummaged under the bed. He came out with Brady's baseball.

"Thanks, pal, I've been looking for that," Brady said happily. "Hey! Do you think we should try it out, just to make sure it still works?"

Hatrick wagged his tail. He loved to play catch with Brady.

"Okay, but just for a minute. I have to get back to cleaning my room," said Brady, as they ran out the door.

Brady soon forgot about cleaning his room, and before he knew it, the weekend was over.

At school on Monday morning, the principal announced that the playground was dry enough to play on.

So at recess, Brady and his friends dropped their pencils, grabbed their gloves, and hurried to play a quick ball game at the far end of the schoolyard.

On their way, they chatted about the upcoming baseball season.

"This year," said Kev, "I'm going to try to hit one homer in every game."

"I'm going to try to pitch a no-hitter," added Brady.

"Chester's going to try not to trip over first base," joked Freddie. Everyone laughed, even Chester.

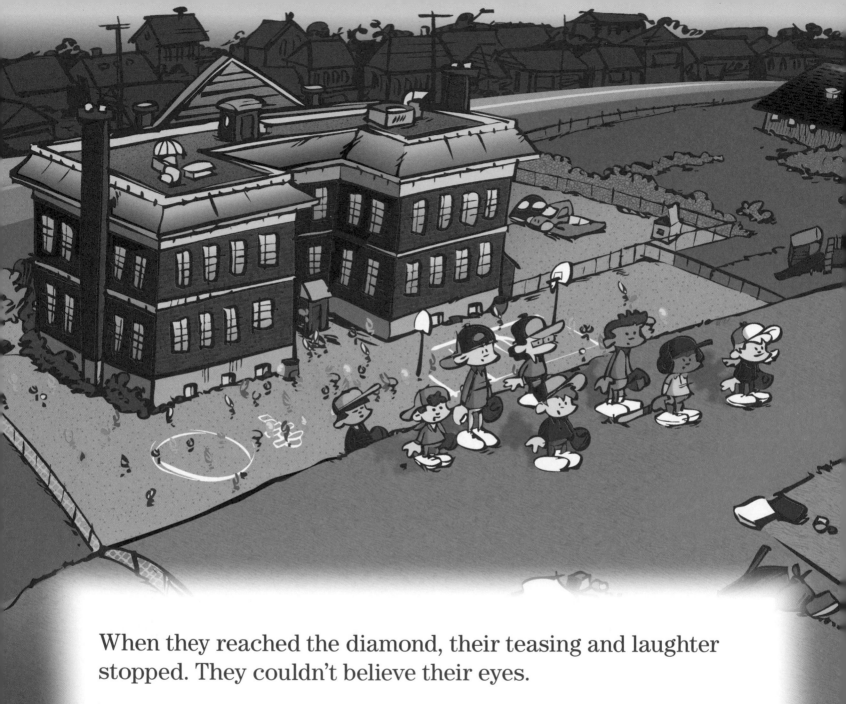

When they reached the diamond, their teasing and laughter stopped. They couldn't believe their eyes.

There was no first base, no home base, and no pitcher's mound. But there was a mound of garbage! Heaps and heaps of garbage everywhere!

"Wow," said Freddie, "what a mess!"

"There must be a ton of garbage," said Chester, wiping his glasses and shaking his head.

"It looks more like a dump than a baseball field," added Caroline, wrinkling her nose.

"What are we going to do?" asked Tree.

Nobody had an answer, but one thing was certain. They wouldn't be playing ball any time soon.

During journal time, Brady's teacher told the class they could write about anything they wanted. But all Brady could think about was the baseball diamond mess.

By the end of the day, Brady still had his room to finish cleaning **and** a journal entry to write for homework. Things were going from bad to worse.

Brady thought about the ball diamond while he walked Hatrick.

He thought about it while he sorted a few more boxes.

He thought about it during dinner. His mom noticed that he wasn't eating. "Brady Brady," she said, "is something bothering you?"

"Yeah," answered Brady sadly. "My friends and I wanted to play baseball today at recess, but we couldn't. There was garbage all over the field."

"It's too bad you couldn't play baseball, but think about how all that garbage might affect the air, the plants, and the animals," said his mom.

"Yeah, Brady Brady," his sister chimed in.

Brady hadn't thought much about animals or the environment. He had only thought about playing baseball.

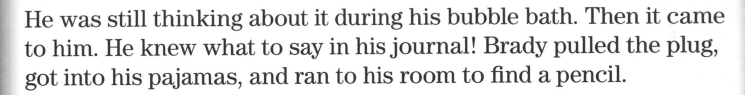

He was still thinking about it during his bubble bath. Then it came to him. He knew what to say in his journal! Brady pulled the plug, got into his pajamas, and ran to his room to find a pencil.

Brady was eager to show his homework to the teacher the next morning.

During sharing time, she called Brady up to the front and asked him to read his journal out loud.

Brady read: "Yesterday, I couldn't play baseball at recess. That made me sad. Then I realized that garbage and stuff left on the ground hurts everybody. I was worried about playing baseball, but I should have been worried about our environment."

When Brady finished, the class was silent. It was unusual that no one had anything to say. That was okay, because Brady had a *great* idea!

At recess, he went straight to the baseball field and got down to work.

Chester was the first to notice Brady. He stopped playing basketball and joined in to help.

Then, Kev, Tree, Freddie, and Caroline noticed Brady and Chester. They stopped playing tag and joined in, too.

Before they knew it, the entire school was pitching in. When the bell rang, they all started walking back to their classrooms.

"It doesn't smell like a dump anymore," said Caroline, looking back over her shoulder.

"It sure was neat how we all pitched in and worked as a team to get the job done," Brady said proudly.

During lunch, the principal's voice came over the PA.

Attention, students. In appreciation of doing such a fine job of cleaning and greening our schoolyard, I am declaring a baseball fun afternoon for the entire school — students against the teachers!

Everyone hurried to gather at the baseball field.

Before Brady threw the first pitch, he led the whole
school in a cheer . . .

We've got the power,
We've got the might,
Our schoolyard was a mess,
So we made it right!

It turned out to be the best schoolyard ball game ever!

On Saturday, Brady was up at the crack of dawn, but not to play baseball. He was determined his room would look as clean as the baseball diamond.

And with a little help from his pal, it wouldn't take long!